Gift of the Curupira

PRAISE FOR *STORYSHARES*

"One of the brightest innovators and game-changers in the education industry."
– Forbes

"Your success in applying research-validated practices to promote literacy serves as a valuable model for other organizations seeking to create evidence-based literacy programs."

- Library of Congress

"We need powerful social and educational innovation, and Storyshares is breaking new ground. The organization addresses critical problems facing our students and teachers. I am excited about the strategies it brings to the collective work of making sure every student has an equal chance in life."
– Teach For America

"Around the world, this is one of the up-and-coming trailblazers changing the landscape of literacy and education."
- International Literacy Association

"It's the perfect idea. There's really nothing like this. I mean wow, this will be a wonderful experience for young people."   - Andrea Davis Pinkney, Executive Director, Scholastic

"Reading for meaning opens opportunities for a lifetime of learning. Providing emerging readers with engaging texts that are designed to offer both challenges and support for each individual will improve their lives for years to come. Storyshares is a wonderful start."
- David Rose, Co-founder of CAST & UDL

Gift of the Curupira

Sergio de Moliere

STORYSHARES

Story Share, Inc.
New York. Boston. Philadelphia

Published in the United States by Story Share, Inc.

The characters and events in this book are fictitious. Any similarity to real persons, living or dead, is entirely coincidental.

Storyshares
Story Share, Inc.
24 N. Bryn Mawr Avenue #340
Bryn Mawr, PA 19010-3304
www.storyshares.org

Inspiring reading with a new kind of book.

Interest Level: High School
Grade Level Equivalent: 2.3

9781642615630

Book design by Storyshares

Printed in the United States of America

Storyshares Presents

1

"Hey, Elena! You're quite the early bird."

"Hi, Jorge. It's the holiday season!" Elena laughed and twirled around.

Jorge grinned. He was short and skinny, with a broad face and black moustache. "You must love school."

Elena shook her head. Her hair bounced like dark springs. It wasn't school she loved—it was Troy.

Jorge checked the wiring on the bulbs. "There will be a big tree for the holiday party, *chica*. Even the teachers are happy."

"I hope you get a big bonus, Jorge. You work so hard."

Jorge grinned and patted Elena on the arm. "I came here from Mexico. We were poor." His mouth twisted into a grimace. "Often, no food. But here, now that I have my green card . . ." He smiled. "It's a paradise. I like to send money back home to Mama." He checked the wiring once more and then left.

In the classroom, Elena hung her coat on a hook and put her bag on the desk. A second later, Troy walked in. He was tall and cute, with wavy red hair and broad shoulders. Elena sighed. He looked like Blake Gray except he was close enough to touch. She wet her lips. She had put on a touch of purple lipstick.

Today, Troy wore his favorite blue shirt. It matched his eyes. Elena was dizzy. As he sat down, his hair fell over his left eye. Yawning, he brushed it away. Elena couldn't breathe. It was crazy. She had no chance with a guy so handsome. But her heart didn't care.

Leaning on her elbows, she set her jaw. Troy was her soulmate. A strong woman always won her guy. And Dominican women were strong women.

Troy yawned again. Elena picked up the cup of coffee she had brought. It was for Troy. She bought one every day just for him. He was always tired and always drank coffee in the morning.

Shaking, she stood and went to his desk.

"Ah, Elena!" Troy ran his hand through his mop of hair. A dimple appeared in his cheek, and Elena's legs went weak.

"Are you okay, babe?" He rubbed his eyes.

"For you." She handed the cup to Troy. Her fingers brushed his, and she was dizzy again. On his right wrist was a blue tattoo of an anchor.

"Mmm, good. I partied last night." He groaned. "I guess I stayed out too late. Do you Mexicans party too?"

Elena raised her chin. "I'm not Mexican. I'm Dominican."

Troy yawned and covered his mouth. His teeth were even and white. "Whatever. I hope you're legal." He laughed.

What does he mean? Elena wondered. *I'm a citizen.*

Troy was older than the other kids. He said he'd been in the navy. As he drank from the cup, his Adam's apple bobbed. Elena's toes curled.

Troy wiped his mouth on his sleeve. "Hit the spot. Thanks, babe."

Elena closed her eyes.

Troy turned on his laptop and began playing Call of Duty.

"Got him!" He jiggled the controls. "Almost as good as the real deal."

"Uh. Troy . . ." Elena played with her hair as Troy stared at the computer. "Troy?" He had forgotten her.

"Go to your seat, Elena. This is no playroom." The English teacher folded her arms. Her mouth was turned down at the corners. Carmen was always angry. Elena didn't like her. It was strange that she never yelled at Troy.

As Elena sat down, Sasha strolled into the room. The pretty girl always made an entrance, as if she was a movie star. Her blonde hair had gold highlights and hung below her waist. She wore a green off the shoulder blouse. Her face was pale and creamy, without any pimples. Elena touched the small one on her own cheek. She frowned. She couldn't stand Sasha.

Swaying her hips, Sasha walked over to Troy. Flashing her teeth, she put her hand on his bicep and squeezed. Troy grinned like crazy.

"You're a real man, honey," Sasha told him.

Troy's cheeks turned red.

Elena looked down. How dumb could she be? She knew she wasn't as pretty as Sasha. The girl was a queen bee and a cheerleader—everything Elena wasn't. Elena touched her hair. It was too curly, and her hips were too big.

Suddenly, Elena's eyes were damp. She ran out of the classroom, right past Carmen. Heading into the bathroom, she locked herself in a stall and cried.

2

That afternoon, Elena took her sandwich to the cafeteria. It was decorated with bright silver tinsel and fresh green holly.

She took a seat alone and, picking up her sandwich, stared at it. She took a small bite. It was baked chicken and ham with hot gravy, melted cheese, lettuce, and tomato. Her favorite. Auntie Alma had made it for her. It was just like the sandwiches from Barra Payan, a restaurant in Santo Domingo.

But Elena couldn't eat. She was sick to her stomach. A few tables away, Sasha sat with Troy. They laughed together and bumped shoulders. Then Troy pulled Sasha to him and kissed her.

Elena bit her lip and made a fist. Under the table, she stamped her foot. She wanted to punch Sasha. She knew it was wrong, but she was mad. Troy was the one Elena loved.

"Hey, Laynee. What's the good word?"

Asim grinned. His teeth were yellow against his copper colored face. He was stocky, and his belly stuck out from the green and white sweater he wore. A Santa hat sat atop his head.

"You're late."

Asim shrugged. "My Mom didn't feel good. Her heart is bad. I had to help her. Besides, I might get in late, but I study like a demon."

"Sure, sure. With you, there's always something." Elena picked up her sandwich, wrinkled her nose, and put it down.

"Hey, Laynee." Asim stared at the sandwich. His mouth watered. "That looks yummy. Nice and greasy too. Mmm. If you're not gonna eat it, I'm pretty hungry."

"I thought you were on a diet," Elena reminded him.

Asim patted his belly. "I've been working out," he said, trying to make a muscle with his arms. "Got to feed these guns."

"Guns? Seriously?" Asim's arms were flabby. She sighed. Troy had big, strong muscles.

"Yep. I want a body like Yul Brynner had. Gee, what a King of Egypt he made!"

"Yule who? You mean like Christmas?"

"No. Yul Brynner. C'mon, Elena, I must have told you about him."

She shook her head.

"He was an actor. He played the King of Egypt in the film *The Ten Commandments*. He took his shirt off a lot." Asim grinned. "I'm gonna have muscles like him if I keep lifting."

Asim knew a lot about actors. "Oh," Elena said, "I thought you wanted to be like Vin Diesel or that bald guy from Star Wars."

Asim nodded. "You mean Lobot. He was part robot. But I also want to be King of Egypt."

Elena made a face.

"Well, I'm Egyptian you know, on my father's side. In his time, Yul was *the man*, although I also like Captain Picard from Star Trek." Asim folded his arms and yelled, "Captain on the bridge!" He sat back in his chair. "*Engage*," he said in a bad British accent.

"Elena," Asim said, "you can be Seven of Nine, and I *insist* you wear black." He moved his dark eyebrows up and down. "You'd be a babe in black!" His eyes glowed.

Elena giggled. Seven of Nine was part robot, and she had a hot bod. She always wore tight body suits. "No way, Asim! You won't catch me in an outfit like that!"

Asim took off his hat and held it to his chest. He didn't have much hair. He had explained to Elena that, as a baby, he got sick and then it didn't grow right.

"I love you, Seven," Asim said, staring into Elena's eyes. "Marry me. I'll be true to you forever and ever. Or at least until the next show." He put his hat back on and stuck out his tongue.

Elena giggled. Asim was a nice guy, but he was too fat and had a hook for a nose. And that hair . . . She shook her head.

"I'm sorry, Captain," Elena said. "I have a boyfriend." She couldn't help looking over at Troy. He was so cute.

Asim stuck his thumb towards Troy. "Oh, *him*. So that loser is the man of your dreams?" He shook his head. "Well, one day you'll know that I'm the better man. Hey, if you won't give me your heart, can you at least give me your sandwich?"

Elena grinned and handed it to him.

Asim ate it all and burped. "Sorry." He patted his belly. "Like a rock. Must have lost five pounds since I started working out. I feel good, too. Hey, Elena, I can't wait for the Christmas party. How about you?"

She nodded.

He snickered. "Maybe I'll even be your Secret Santa again."

Elena rolled her eyes. "Two years in a row? That would be a record."

"The luck of the bold." He smirked.

"Hey, do you have the inside track or what? I think it's rigged."

"Me? Inside track?" He rolled his eyes. "No way. It's just fate."

Elena checked her cell. "Well, that's it for me."

"Leaving so early?" Asim asked. "We have another class."

"I know, but I'm not feeling well. Besides, the nurse said it was okay." She glanced at Troy, but he was joking with Sasha.

Asim lifted an eyebrow. "Oh. I get it."

"There's nothing to get. My stomach's upset."

"If you say so. That Sasha is a piece of work. Not my type though. I don't go for blondes. I think she's divorced."

"Divorced? She's not even twenty."

Asim sighed. "She's a bad girl." He shook his head. "Well, Seven, I've got to study. Even the King of Egypt needs good grades. See ya."

Elena grinned. It was weird. Troy was her soulmate, but Asim made her laugh.

She walked over to the elevator. Her stomach was still upset as she left the building. She took the subway and got off at Bedford Avenue, a few stops from her own Bushwick neighborhood. She'd never been to Bedford Avenue before. Aunt Alma said it was an area for rich college kids. But Elena was curious. She heard there were cute shops and bookstores nearby.

Stopping at a window, she stared at the covers of romance novels. She blushed. The men on the covers wore no shirts. Elena dreamed of writing her own romance novel. Troy would be on the cover without a shirt. Her cheeks burned hotter. She walked faster. Maybe she wanted too much, but she couldn't help it.

Elena stopped near a crowd. A group of people in their early twenties stood outside a bar. Most held beers or glasses of wine. Loud music blasted onto the street. Elena recognized a Beyoncé song. Despite the cold, a young guy with bleached hair wore a muscle shirt and black leather pants. He had dragon tattoos on his bare arms.

"Hey, Latina, want a drink? On me."

Elena shook her head. "I don't drink."

"C'mon," he yelled. "You afraid of immigration? I'll keep you safe."

Elena hurried off. She knew she didn't belong here.

Elena turned down Lorimer street, away from the bars on Bedford Avenue. She took long strides, pumping her stiff legs. She kept seeing the image of Troy kissing Sasha. When she thought of it, her chest ached.

Soon, she was lost. She checked her cell, but there was no signal. The streets were empty, and many of the stores were boarded up.

Elena slowed down. It was overcast and began to sleet. The icy drops slammed against her cheeks. She shivered, pulling her coat tight around her and looking for street signs.

At the corner was an odd storefront, the faded sign cracked and yellow. A worn flag hung from a pole. It was the Dominican flag—a white cross in the center and four squares, two red and two dark blue. Dull letters on the sign spelled *Libreria Communitaria*. It was local book store.

Elena pressed her nose to the window, but it was too dusty to see inside. Lightning blazed and thunder boomed. Then the sleet fell harder. Elena shivered and went into the store.

It was dim and musty inside. An old woman sat behind the counter. She blinked. Her eyes were dull. She was tiny, with long orange hair. Her face was brown and worn like leather.

"Hi," said Elena in a small voice. "Are you open?"

The woman nodded and waved a crooked hand. Her nails were long and pointed.

Elena brushed water off her coat and looked around. Dirty shelves were filled with dark books. Strange pictures in red and black hung on the wall behind the register. On one, a demon with rusty skin sat cross-legged in a jungle. The trees around her were bent, their branches twisted. The sky was dark violet, and the moon was black.

The demon by the tree had bright red hair that coiled like a snake. Her teeth were sharp and yellow. Elena shivered. She recognized the *Curupira*, a Dominican demon who tortured men and stole children.

The old woman laughed hoarsely. She pointed a bony finger at a table in the back of the room. Elena felt her feet move towards it. She stopped in front of a large, thick book. The book cover was black with odd silver symbols. Elena opened it. A gust of wind stirred the pages. They were stiff, like old parchment.

Gray dust rose in the air. Elena sneezed and wiped her eyes. She stared at the lettering. The words were written in red ink. They were in a kind of Spanish that was hard for Elena to read. She narrowed her eyes. A few words were familiar. It was a recipe for a love potion!

The old woman came up behind Elena. With a swift motion, her bony hand ripped out the page. She offered it to Elena.

"For me?" Elena blinked. "A gift?"

The woman grunted. Her orange hair brushed the floor. Elena stood for a moment. Then she took it.

As soon as she grabbed the paper, the old woman bared her teeth. They were dark and sharp like fangs. Turning, the woman limped back to the counter. Her feet made heavy, scratching noises on the floor.

Elena choked as she noticed the old woman's feet. They were turned backwards. They were not the feet of a person but the feet of the Dominican demon in the picture. The *Curupira*! Elena tried to swallow, but her mouth was dry.

The old woman glared at her. Then she laughed. The sound was awful, like metal chains rubbing against a blackboard. Elena screamed and ran from the store.

Outside, the sleet had turned to cold rain. It was dark as midnight, as if Elena had been in the bookstore for hours. She heard a noise behind her and began running. Elena ran for three blocks before she stopped. Scared and out of breath, she rushed down to the subway. Her hand still clutched the dusty parchment.

Gift of the Curupira

3

Alma sat on the carpet with her hands on her thighs. Her black hair was up in a bun, and she wore a pale pink jump suit. Behind Alma was a large Christmas tree. On top was a cheery gold and silver angel with white wings.

Alma loved Christmas. She had pinned green and red stockings up on the wall. An oil painting of Santa and Mrs. Claus hung over the fake brick fireplace. Red and yellow lights flashed as if a real fire burned.

Elena stepped inside slowly. She was cold and damp. She watched as Alma stretched and touched her nose to the ground. As always, Elena was impressed by her aunt's yoga skills. Despite Alma's age, she practiced yoga every day, plus twenty minutes of meditation. Her body was thin, and her face was smooth. Elena thought of Sasha's slim body and knew that she must also do yoga.

Alma looked up as Elena sneezed.

"Hi, Alma."

"Are you ill? What is that in your hand?" Alma cocked her head.

Elena shivered. She didn't realize she still had the parchment. It was crumpled in her fist.

"Huh? This? Nothing." She hid her hand behind her back.

"You think I am blind, *chica*? Come, show me. A page held so tight must have importance, no? Show me please."

Elena slowly handed her aunt the parchment.

Alma put on her glasses and unfolded the stiff paper. "Hmm, such coarse paper and yellow with age." She stared at the writing, and her body jerked. "*Dios mío!* It is written in *castellano antiguo*, old Spanish." Alma covered her mouth with her hand and stared at Elena. "*Dios!* It is the black magic—the worst kind. The spell of a witch or a demon."

She looked at Elena. "A love potion?" Alma frowned and stared at the parchment again. "This is ancient, foul work. It is cursed." Her eyes darkened. "Where did you get this black magic, *chica?*"

"I–I just found it," Elena lied. She held out her hand. "Please give it back."

Alma frowned and touched the page with slim fingers. She traced the symbols. "A love potion? What does a pretty girl like you need with such a thing, hmm?"

Alma shook her head. "This recipe will do you no good. And these symbols . . ." She studied them for a moment. "*Jesucristo!* It is the work of a *Curupira*, an awful demon. The black magic of a *Curupira* is an evil thing. I must throw this parchment out now, *chica*, while I still can."

Elena didn't move, but every muscle in her body was tight. She wanted the recipe for the love potion. Needed it. Her fingers itched, and she clenched and unclenched her hands. The image of Troy's face rose in her mind—his dimpled chin and sky-blue eyes. She held out both arms, and her hands shook. "Please, Alma. Please. Give it back to me."

Her aunt's face was hard. "No." Alma took a long, deep breath and exhaled slowly. "No, no, I do not think so."

Elena trembled. Her fingers curled as if trying to touch the parchment.

Alma studied her niece. "Ah," Alma said. "I see you want it very much, this page of the black magic." Raising her arm, Alma held the parchment up in the air, waving it. "So, maybe I will give it back to you. Maybe."

For a moment, Alma held it out to Elena. But as Elena reached for it, her aunt withdrew her hand, shaking her head. "Yet it is cursed."

Elena bit her lip. She didn't know what to do. As Alma stared at Elena, Alma's shoulders began to shake. Her mouth twisted, as if she was having a fit. Elena cried out.

A moment later, Alma's dark eyes twinkled, and she rocked with laughter. "*Dios mío, bonita.* You are educated in America and yet you still believe in this Dominican bull?"

"No, I just . . ." Elena's cheeks burned.

Alma laughed so hard she almost fell over. Elena stamped her foot. She hated it when Alma made fun of her. Although born in the Dominican Republic, her aunt had a master's degree and a wicked sense of humor.

"Okay, okay. *Por favor,* please. Elena, take it before I die from laughing." Alma held the parchment out to Elena, who grabbed it back.

Alma gulped air and tried to calm herself. "*Caramba*, my beloved niece needs a magic love potion?" She groaned. "Who is the lucky man?"

Elena's face was hot. "A guy at school. Troy. He's . . . he's amazing, Alma! Handsome with wavy hair. And he's hardworking. And his eyes, Alma. So blue, like the sky."

"*Pobrecita*. You are lovesick, then? Ah well, then perhaps you need this potion. Who knows? It might get you what you want."

"Really?"

Alma rolled her eyes.

Elena's words came out in a rush. "The old woman who gave it to me had orange hair and backwards feet. A real *Curupira*. It has to work."

"Ha! Orange hair and backwards feet? The demon *Curupira* itself spoke to you? Where was this?"

Elena nodded. "In a bookstore in Williamsburg. She didn't speak. She just gave me the love potion. A gift, I think."

"I see. A gift from a *Curupira*." Alma sighed. "You are sure the woman had backwards feet, huh?"

"She did. I saw it, Alma. I saw it with my own eyes. She limped and had long orange hair and backwards feet. She really was a *Curupira*. I'm sure of it. She must have known that I'm in love and need it."

Alma took a breath. "Ah. This young man at school, this Troy. Does he know your feelings, Elena? Does he care for you?"

Elena tossed her hair. Her lips trembled. "I don't know."

"Yes. I see now what this is. Come here, *chica*." Alma took Elena's hand. "You are cold, *chica*. I will warm you." Alma rubbed Elena's hand, and Elena felt energy move from her aunt into her own body.

After a minute, Alma sighed. "I should not have made fun of you. It was wrong. It's just . . . we women can be fools for love. I feel I have sheltered you too much from life, from romance. You are a dreamer." She patted Elena's hand. "So, do you really love him, this boy at school?"

Elena hesitated. "I think so." Her voice was faint. "He's the one who makes me dizzy with love."

"I see. Well, perhaps the magic love potion will work." Alma sighed. "You are still a child."

"I'm sixteen going on seventeen. I'm not a child," Elena said. "I'm all grown up."

Alma smiled. "Of course. As you wish, child. Now, come." She rose to her feet, still holding Elena's hand. "Let us go to dinner. My stomach growls, and soon she will bite." She kissed Elena on the cheek. "Later, I will help my sweet grown-up niece with her love potion."

Gift of the Curupira

4

Alma cooked a dinner of fresh meat stew called *sancocho*, with white rice and *tostones* (fried plantains). Even after twenty years in America, Alma still liked homemade Dominican food, except on Thanksgiving and Christmas. On those days, she cooked American meals.

Spicy aromas filled the air as Elena's aunt stood at the stove, frying the *tostones*. Alma stirred the stew and inhaled.

"*Dios*, Elena! It smells so good I drool like a dog."

Elena helped lay out the dishes and spoons. Her aunt gave them both hearty helpings of the hot food.

"It's too much food," Elena whined, talking with a full mouth. She wanted to eat less so she could start losing weight. However, the tasty food was hard to resist. She didn't refuse when Alma heaped more onto her plate.

Once again she admired her aunt, who ate like a horse yet stayed slim. Elena didn't want to end up with a belly like Asim. Of course, he was a man, so it wasn't the same thing. Besides, even Asim had started to work out.

After dinner, Alma sipped coffee while Elena drank tea. Despite her aunt's love of yoga, she favored the traditional Dominican *caffecita* over tea. When they finished their drinks, they went into the living room. Alma sank down into lotus pose. Elena tried to copy her. Soon, her thighs hurt too much, and she gave up. She stretched her legs out and rubbed them.

Alma studied the parchment and helped Elena translate the old Spanish. Soon, she had written the ingredients of the love potion in English. There were eleven that had to be mixed. Then the mixture needed to "settle" for a day or two until the potion was at full strength.

"You had better make your own list," Alma advised, "in case the writing disappears, or the magic parchment burns with fire."

Elena thought Alma was joking. Still, it didn't hurt to be safe. Taking out her laptop, she typed up the ingredients.

1. *aloe vera*

2. *egg yolk from a black hen*

3. *pinch of salt*

4. *rooster's crow*

5. *rum*

6. *red wine*

7. *honey*

8. *tree bark/root mix*

9. *agave*

10. *grated tortoise shell*

11. *Mama juana*

Elena rubbed her eyes. So many things. Aloe vera was easy to get, as was salt, rum, red wine, and honey. But she wasn't sure about *agave*.

"That is no problem." Alma told her that *agave* was made from the tequila plant. "If nothing else, that plus the rum and red wine will get your young man drunk."

Elena nodded but didn't laugh. This was important. "What about the tree bark/root mix and the marijuana? Where can I get those?"

Alma grinned. "Not marijuana. *Mama juana*. It is *no problema*. *Mama juana* is a mix of herbs. They sell it along with tree bark/root mix at Dominican drug stores in Washington Heights. The dry mix has to be blended with the red wine and rum," Alma advised.

"And the grated tortoise shell," Elena asked. "Must we kill a turtle?"

Alma snorted. "No, my *chica*. Often the best *mama juana* will have that too."

"How do you know all this, Auntie?"

Now it was Alma's turn to blush. "I was a child once too, *chica*." She shrugged. "I use some in my cooking.

Also, the young man I loved was an herb expert. He did research on herbs and went to far off places to collect them."

"You never married him, Auntie?"

"No. I broke his heart. He left. No marriage; no children. Instead, a degree from university. You are my only child, Elena."

"Never even engaged?"

"Almost. My young man gave me the knee. I was *estupida*—dumb. I did not know his value. I judged his appearance too harshly. Oh *chica*, not everything is in the looks.

"You refused him?"

"Yes. A foolish girl turned down a nice young man to wait for the handsome one who never stayed."

Elena hugged Alma. "I'm so sorry, Auntie."

Alma sighed. "That was a long time ago. Now, let's finish your recipe."

Elena was excited. "We will have almost everything. I will just need the egg yolk from a black hen and the crow of a rooster."

"I don't know, child. I think you must go to a farm for those," said Alma, scratching her head. "That is *muy extraño*—very strange. Those things are the most magical parts of the recipe. Thank goodness the recipe did not ask you to strangle the rooster and chew up its head."

Elena made a face. "I think Asim's uncle has a farm in New Jersey."

"Asim?"

Elena nodded. "The Egyptian guy I know from school. You met him once. He's fat with a round face and a big smile. He jokes a lot."

"Ah. I remember him now. A nice young man. Are you sure he will help?"

Elena smiled. "Asim would do anything for me."

"Ah. I see." Alma frowned. "Well, even if you make the potion, how will you give it to your Troy?"

Elena smiled. "That part is easy. I bring coffee for Troy every day. With the two lumps of sugar he likes, he won't notice when I put in the potion." She giggled.

Alma shook her head. "That is a part of my niece I do not know."

Elena laughed. "I want Troy to love me by Christmas." She needed Troy to be with her at the school Christmas party. Just the thought of kissing Troy under the mistletoe made her cheeks hot.

Alma wagged a finger. "Oh, Elena, you wiggle like a worm and glow with the light of the solar lanterns from the Dominican Republic. Be calm, *chica*. You do not know if this potion will work. Magic does not follow orders, especially black magic."

Elena shook her head. She knew it would work.

Suddenly, she put down the parchment and blew on her hands. They were warm. She held them up. Would they burst into flame? She stared at Alma. Her aunt said nothing, but her eyes were dark.

Gift of the Curupira

5

Asim chewed a pastrami sandwich. He sat with Elena in the cafeteria and wrinkled his nose. Then he licked mayonnaise off his fingers.

"I don't get it, Elena. Why do you ask if my uncle has a black hen? What difference does it make if a hen is black or white? It's the eggs that matter. Anyway, you can buy eggs in the supermarket."

"Well, I read that eggs from black hens are special."

Asim took another bite of the sandwich. He gulped down the food before answering. "No, that's not true. Eggs are eggs. They all have fat unless they're from a vegan hen. My uncle's hens are not vegan. Worse, they're all fowl." Asim almost choked on the food as he laughed at his own joke.

"Stop it! I mean it, Asim. This is important to me. I need an egg from a black hen, and I need it soon." Elena drummed her fingers on the table. She didn't want to tell Asim why she needed the egg, but by the look on his face, he suspected something.

Asim grew serious. "Okay. If it matters to you, Elena, it matters to me." He wiped his mouth. "Yes, my uncle has a black hen. In fact, he has several black hens, a few white ones, and even a couple speckled brown. What gives, Elena? Why the sudden interest in chickens?"

Elena sat back in her chair. She hadn't touched her food. "I'll tell you if you promise not to make jokes or laugh."

Asim nodded and pursed his lips. Elena knew he could be serious when it counted. Asim was bright as well as funny. Elena noticed that his jawline was visible. He actually was losing weight. He had also trimmed his hair.

"Okay." Asim rested his chin on his hands. "Just tell me the truth. I promise not to make any jokes. Why is the black hen so important?"

"It's for a love potion. Egg yolk from a black hen is one of the ingredients."

"A love potion." He made a face. "Oh geez. It's for Troy, isn't it?"

She nodded.

"Cripe, Elena. You're crazy about that Irish dude. Give it a rest."

Elena was furious. "You promised not to make fun of me!"

"I'm sorry, I'm sorry." Asim sighed. "Okay. A love potion. An egg from a black hen is one of the ingredients. It's a recipe?"

"Right." Elena paused, then blurted out the rest. "I got the recipe from an old woman with backwards feet— a witch—in a bookstore in Williamsburg. I need the egg yolk from a black hen."

Asim licked his lips. "Now wait a minute. Let me get this straight. You went to a bookstore in Williamsburg, and an ugly old woman with backwards feet gave you a love potion?"

"Yes, but she didn't give me a love potion. She gave me a recipe for one. And I didn't say she was ugly."

"You implied she was ugly. You said a witch."

"Okay, okay. She was ugly with long orange hair and a crazy laugh. And backwards feet."

"Backwards feet? An ugly witch with backwards feet? Why are they backwards? That's ridiculous. "

"It's not ridiculous, Asim. It's a Dominican demon. We call her the *Curupira.*"

"Okay. An ugly witch with backwards feet told you to get an egg from a black hen and other ingredients."

"Yes. Only she didn't tell me. She gave me the recipe on parchment."

He narrowed his eyes. "Okay. She gave you the recipe on parchment. So you need a black hen. What are the other ingredients?"

Elena folded her arms. "Why do you need to know? Does it matter?"

"Of course it matters. Gee, Elena. If I'm going to help you, I need to know everything."

"Okay, okay." She nodded, then described the other ingredients.

"I see." Asim scratched his chin. There was a lot of dark stubble.

"You need to shave," Elena blurted.

"What's that part about a rooster? Tell me again." Asim scratched his chin harder.

"You really need a shave, Asim."

"Let's pretend I'm growing a beard. Now tell me the rooster thing."

"Okay." Elena took a breath. "In addition to everything else, I need the crow of a rooster."

"The toe of a rooster?"

"No, not the toe, the crow."

"The crow?"

"Yes. The crow, not the toe." Elena screwed up her face.

"That's what I thought you said. The crow of a rooster." Asim frowned. "Are you sure it's not the *crop* of a rooster?"

"The *crop*? What's a crop? I'm pretty sure it's a crow, not a crop." Elena rubbed her eyes. "It was in Spanish, Asim. The recipe was in Spanish."

"In Spanish? Then how do you know it was a *crow* and not a *toe* or a *crop*? You told me you don't know Spanish that well."

"I don't. Alma translated it for me."

"Oh, your aunt."

"Yes. Spanish is her first language. She's very smart, Asim. If she said it was a *crow*, it must be a crow, not a *crop*. Anyway, what's a *crop*? I never heard of it. How's that different from a *crow*?"

Asim grinned. "You are one confused lady. Haven't you ever been to a farm?"

Elena shook her head. "I was raised in Brooklyn."

"Look, Elena. Hens and roosters have what's called a crop. It's a pouch, kind of like a second little stomach."

"Don't be so smug. So a crop is a little stomach?"

"Yes. Of course, it's also something you plant. For instance, my uncle grows crops on the farm."

"Stop it, Asim. Now you're being funny."

"Sorry, sorry. Couldn't help it."

Elena was getting tense. "So what's a crow? Is it anything like a crop?"

"No, Elena. It's nothing like a crop. A crow is not a crop. A crow is a black bird."

"No, no, no! Stop playing games. What's a rooster's *crow*? Is it a special kind of crop? Or a special kind of bird?"

"No. It's nothing like a crop or a bird. A crow is the sound a rooster makes."

"A sound? I don't understand. First you said it was a stomach. Then you said it was a bird."

"I never said it was a stomach. A *crop* is a stomach. A *crow* is a bird, but it's also a sound. A rooster's crow. Gee, Elena, don't you know anything about barnyard animals? Like when they say, 'the rooster crows'?"

Elena slapped her hands on her thighs. "Now I'm all confused. I've heard that, but it doesn't make any sense. I get it that the rooster crows. Are you sure it's not a kind of a crop? It said a rooster's crow."

"Yes. It's nothing like a crop. It's a noise. Like *cock-a-doodle doo.* That's the rooster's crow. It's not a bird."

"Stop making jokes."

"I'm not. I'm serious. That's what a rooster's crow is. It's not a bird, and it's not a stomach. It's a sound a rooster makes."

"Great, Asim. That's no help. That makes no sense at all. How can I put a sound into a love potion?" Elena pulled at her hair. Maybe the *Curupira* had made a fool out of her after all. A fool for love like Alma said.

Asim rubbed his neck. "Wait a minute. The recipe requires a rooster's crow?"

"Yes. I told you."

Asim wrinkled his forehead. "A rooster's crow."

"Yes, in addition to the other ten ingredients. You have to put them all together."

"Wait. Ten ingredients *plus* a rooster's crow. It's a magic potion. I think I get it. You don't put the sound *into* the recipe. You need the sound *while* you're mixing the other ingredients. It's not just about the ingredients. It's about the time."

"The time? I don't get it." Elena's head ached, and they were going to be late for class.

"Listen, Elena. A rooster crows at dawn. It's a magic potion, right? You have to mix the ingredients at dawn when the rooster crows."

"Oh."

Asim grinned. "Exactly. It makes sense. See, Elena, that's why I needed to know everything. Magic potions often are made at special times of the day or night. This one has to be made at dawn when the rooster crows."

"Ha! Yes. It does make sense now." Elena sighed. So, she wasn't a fool after all.

"Fist bump, Laynee." Asim held up his fist.

Elena grinned and held up her fist. Asim bumped it lightly. His fist was large and warm. For some reason, the contact made Elena feel funny.

They got up and hurried to class. When Elena passed Troy, she waved and smiled. "Hey, Troy," she called out. Then she giggled.

For once, it was the handsome Irishman who was tongue tied.

6

Elena wrote in her journal. She sat across from Alma, who was knitting a wool scarf.

"Soon, you will have a new red scarf for Christmas, Elena," Alma announced. She held up the scarf and examined it. "Yes, this will look very good around your pretty neck. Also, it matches your blouse."

Elena crossed out the last line and frowned. "I wanted to write you a poem, but it's not working. I wish I could knit," she said. "Then I could make you a scarf, too." Alma had once tried to teach her, but Elena was all thumbs.

"My niece here for Christmas is all the gift I need," said Alma. "Although if you want to write a poem to me, that is fine too." She smiled. "Santa has been very good to me, child."

Alma knitted a few more loops then looked up. "How are you doing with the *Curupira's* gift—the magic love potion? Do you have all the ingredients yet?"

Elena nodded. She wasn't sure if Alma would like the plan. "I have gotten almost everything I need. I was confused with the rooster's crow."

"Ah yes, a strange thing."

"Yes, but it's fine now. Asim figured it out." Elena explained how Asim had come up with the answer to the problem.

Alma was amazed that Asim had figured it out. "This Asim must be a wizard. Are you sure he doesn't have backwards feet?"

Elena shot Alma a look.

"Well, *chica*, he is a very clever young man. He is not by chance Dominican, is he?"

"No, Alma, he's Egyptian."

"Ah. This is good. The history of Egypt is of a very smart people who built the pyramids. This Asim comes from good family." She stopped knitting for a moment. "Are you sure he's not your soulmate?"

"No, of course not. That's silly. Asim's just a friend. He's fat and plain. It's Troy who I love." She sighed. "If you met Troy, you'd understand. Troy is amazing. He's so handsome. He's perfect."

Alma sighed.

"Yes, Auntie. I have almost all the ingredients," Elena continued. "Asim is going to get the egg yolk from a black hen on his uncle's farm. But I need to be there too. Early in the morning, when the rooster crows, we will mix everything together. So I'll have to go and stay overnight. A little road trip. Uh, did I mention the farm's in New Jersey? Way out in the boonies."

Alma nodded. "I see. Saturday night. A little road trip to a farm in New Jersey. Way out in the boonies."

"Uh-huh."

"So you will go with Asim up to his uncle's farm and stay overnight?"

Elena nodded, opening her journal.

"And you forgot to tell me about this until now, yes?"

Elena lowered her eyes. "I wasn't sure you'd like the idea of a sleepover."

Alma put down her knitting. "I see. A sleepover. Yes. A sleepover on Saturday night at the farm of Asim's uncle?"

"Yes. A sleepover. Just for one night."

"A sleepover with Asim, not with your beloved Troy?"

"Of course. Troy doesn't know anything about the love potion." She smiled. "It's a secret. So the sleepover is with Asim." She looked at Alma. "Why are you staring at me like that?"

Alma smacked her lips. "Nothing. Okay. So you will pack your night clothes and toothbrush for the sleepover with Asim."

Elena blushed. "The sleepover is not *with* Asim. It's at his uncle's farm."

"I see. So, they have a place for you to sleep at this farm of Asim's uncle?"

Elena ran her hand through her hair. "I think so. Asim said he'll talk to his uncle and work it all out."

"I see. Asim will work it all out. This sleepover. That is very nice of the young man. Will he sleep there too?"

Elena shrugged. "I guess. His uncle must have an extra room or a cot or something. I told you. Asim likes me. It's no biggie."

"Sure. Asim likes you. No biggie."

"Asim will pick me up in the car this evening and drive me there."

"Asim will pick you up in the car and drive you there." Alma said the words slowly, as if she was chewing on them. "So Asim has a car?"

Elena nodded. "Yes. Asim has a car. He saves money since he lives with his mom. She's not well, so Asim takes care of her and saves his money. "

Alma nodded. "I see. Asim takes care of his mom and saves his money."

"Yes. Please stop repeating everything I say. Are you making fun of me?"

Alma waved a hand, as if dismissing the question. Her eyes were big and round. "No, *chica*. I am trying to understand is all. My English is not so good."

"Oh, Alma. Your English is a lot better than my Spanish." Elena sat back in the chair. "So Asim is driving me to the farm, and we'll sleep over. Then in the morning we'll mix the love potion when the rooster crows. When the potion is ready, I will put it in Troy's coffee. Then, at the Christmas party, everything will be wonderful." She tossed her hair.

Alma clucked. "Your hair is getting long, Elena. It is beautiful, my niece, like mink. Soon it will brush the ground like the *Curupira's*."

Elena laughed. "I think Troy likes women with long hair, so I want to grow it long." She paused and frowned, fingering her curls. "Sasha has long hair, but it's blonde."

"Sasha? Who's Sasha? Tell me about this Sasha."

Elena twisted her mouth. "She's just a girl at school. A pretty blond who flirts with Troy."

"This pretty blond, she is your age?"

"Oh no. Sasha's older, at least eighteen or nineteen. I think she's divorced. At least that's what Asim says. She's very pretty, but Asim doesn't like her."

"I see. So, this pretty blond Asim does not like flirts with your Troy. And what does your Troy think of this Sasha?"

"How should I know?" Elena frowned, tugging at her hair. "Troy is a guy. He doesn't know Sasha like I do. She's evil, Alma. Sasha's not good for Troy. She makes eyes at Troy and wiggles her body like this." Elena shook her hips and pushed out her chest. "She's an evil woman."

Alma laughed. "You do that well with the hips, my niece. Hips don't lie."

Elena rolled her eyes.

Alma nodded. "Yes, I see. An evil woman, this Sasha. She makes with the hips." Alma paused a moment. "The *Curupira* is an evil woman too, no? Yet you use her potion?"

"Yes, Alma, but that's not the same thing. Gee, why must you ask all these questions?"

Alma's eyes were wide. "No reason, *chica*. I try to understand. That is all. My love for you is great, little one, a big love. I wish for you to be happy."

"I know." Elena gave Alma a hug. "I want to be happy too. That's why I need the love potion. Now, let me get everything packed before Asim gets here."

7

When Asim honked the horn, Elena went to the window and waved.

"He's here! I have to run," Elena told Alma.

"I thought he would come up. I would like to talk to him."

Elena shook her head. "Sorry, Alma. Asim wants to get there before dark. Maybe next time."

"Will there be a next time?"

Elena blew her aunt a kiss. Then, grabbing her bag, she hurried downstairs. Asim was double-parked near the front of the building.

"Got all the ingredients?"

Elena nodded as she got in the passenger seat. Asim's car was an old gray Chevy, but the seats were cozy. In a moment, they were headed down the street.

Elena was impressed. Asim did not stop at the entrance to the highway. Instead, he sped up and merged easily into the lane. The engine made a funny noise when he hit fifty but, except for a little vibration, there was no problem.

"She's old, but I take good care of her," Asim said, patting the steering wheel. "Ain't that right, Elena?"

"Elena? You call the car Elena?"

"Yep. It didn't feel right talking to the old girl without knowing her name."

"That's my name," Elena protested.

"I named it after Elena Gilbert from the Vampire Diaries. Nina Dobrev played the role, and she was pretty." Asim grinned.

"I suppose. She has dark hair though."

Asim nodded. "Just the kind of hair I like. Dark and soft. Kind of like yours."

Elena squirmed in the seat.

"How do you know the car's a girl?" Elena demanded. She was upset, but she wasn't sure why.

Asim patted the dashboard. "Elena's a girl alright. A guy just knows."

Asim turned on the music. "Do you like Nora Jones?"

Elena was startled. "She's great."

"This is from her first album."

"Oh, I love this song! I didn't know you liked her."

"Surprised?" Asim grinned but kept his eyes on the road.

"A little. I thought you liked heavy metal. Never guessed you were a Nora Jones fan."

"She's cute with dark hair. I'm into her now. It's a new kind of music for me. I'm trying to move into other things. Music, exercise. It's all part of my master plan. Weight lifting and good food for my body. Music for my soul. I'm reading more too, for my mind."

"I'm impressed."

"Yep. The more you get to know me, the more impressed you'll be. You read a lot, don't you, Elena?"

She nodded. "I write, too." She paused then blurted it out. "One day I hope to publish my work."

"Seriously?" Asim whistled. "Now *I'm* impressed."

Asim drove for another twenty minutes as Elena leaned back, stared out the window, and listened to Nora Jones. It was very nice. She had become drowsy when she was jolted awake as Asim made a sharp turn. The car shook as the ground became rough.

"Sorry about that. The path gets bumpy once we're off the highway." He peered out the window. "There, it's the next dirt path on the right. Yeah, I know, but it's a farm."

Asim turned on the headlights, and shadows leaped in front of the car as they moved. It was getting dark. He drove slowly for a few more minutes, then a shadowed shape bounded in front of the car. He slammed on the brakes. Elena jerked forward but was stopped by the seatbelt.

"Darn!" Asim rubbed his face.

"Was that a deer?" Elena asked.

He nodded. "Lucky I have good reflexes," he said as they began moving again.

As he turned another corner, he glanced at her. "Just in time," he said, pulling into a driveway. "Home sweet home."

He parked the car, and they got out. It was pitch black.

"You see the little cabin off to the far right?" He pointed into the darkness.

"I'm not sure." Elena hugged herself. It was not only dark, it was getting colder by the minute.

"I should have warned you. The temperature drops at night out here. That little cabin is where we'll be sleeping. Don't worry though. There's a heater and nice thick blankets. The main house is about a quarter mile away."

He pointed in the opposite direction. "See the large building with the Christmas reindeer in front and the Christmas lights on the front porch? That's where my uncle and aunt live. We probably won't see them until tomorrow. They get up at 4:30am, so they're probably getting ready for bed now."

"It's so quiet." Elena was used to city noise. Except for the crickets and a low buzzing, it was as silent as a cemetery.

"Yes. It takes some getting used to," Asim said, taking a deep breath. "Once you do, you'll love it." He inhaled again. "Just smell that fresh air. The air here's a lot cleaner and healthier than in the city. Living out here also builds up your appetite." He shrugged. "My uncle eats like a pig, but he's as solid as a rock and as strong as a bull. Me, I'm a work in progress."

Elena was quiet. This was a different Asim than the funny guy she had known for the past year and a half. In the darkness, he was solid and dependable.

He led the way toward the cabin, taking out a pocket flashlight. "The ground's uneven, so be careful where you step."

She nodded. A moment later, she stumbled. She cried out when Asim startled her by putting his arm around her shoulders to steady her.

"Sorry," he muttered, withdrawing.

Elena said nothing. She was stunned by the shivery feeling passing up and down her body.

"Wow. Look at that moon." Asim stopped and stared at the sky. A huge golden balloon hung in the sky, surrounded by tiny jewels in the velvet blackness.

"It doesn't look real," Elena said. "Like someone hung up a lantern."

"It's real all right. It's a harvest moon. Pretty common out here during Christmas time. You just don't see a moon like that in the city. Romantic, isn't it?"

Elena took a breath. She wished Alma was with her.

Asim sighed. "Look at all those stars. The Christmas story about the star makes more sense out here." He sang softly, "*A star, a star, shining in the night with a tail as big as a kite.*"

Asim had a nice baritone voice, even though he was a little off key. Elena began walking faster. She didn't understand the waves of emotion passing through her or the tightness in her chest.

8

The trek in the dark took longer than she thought. At last, they reached the cabin. There were three steps that led to the front door. Asim opened it and turned on the lights.

"It's nice and cozy. That's the kitchen," he said, inclining his head towards a small alcove to the left. The bedroom's in the back. That's where we'll sleep."

"Asim . . ."

"No worries, Elena. I didn't mean we'd sleep *together*. There are two twin beds." He grunted.

There was a funny expression on his face. "There's also a screen I can move between the beds if you're worried. I'm a gentleman." He laughed. "Not that I wouldn't mind seeing you in your cute nightie."

"Uh . . ."

"Just joking." Asim turned away and went into the kitchen.

Elena was silent. She felt a little guilty. Did Asim want more than just friendship?

She suddenly realized the implications of this trip. Her throat was dry, and she swallowed. Jesus! She was alone in this isolated cabin with Asim, a young guy who had a crush on her. They'd be sleeping in the same room. She'd be in bed in her nightgown, just inches away from him. A sleepover, she had called it. No wonder Alma reacted like that. How naive could she be? Blushing, she wondered if Asim had a box of condoms in his pocket.

Asim came out of the kitchen with two small trays of muffins and cocoa. "I don't know about you, Elena, but I could use a hot drink and a little snack. These are homemade blueberry muffins. My aunt baked them."

He put the trays down on a small table. "You can just sit down on the sofa over there. Let me take your things. I'll put them in the bedroom."

Elena nodded, and Asim went into the bedroom. She took her tray, sat on the couch, and sipped the warm drink. She took a bite of the muffin. It was delicious. When the cup of cocoa was half empty, her eyelids were already getting heavy.

Asim came out of the bedroom and hurried into the kitchen. He exited a few minutes later, rosy cheeked and bursting with energy. "Elena? Locked and loaded! I've put the love potion ingredients in the kitchen. We'll be all ready to go in the morning." Asim picked up a tray and sat down next to her.

She blinked, trying not to nod off.

"Are you okay? I thought maybe we'd catch a movie or listen to music. We're backwards up here in the boonies but not that backward." His eyes were bright, and he edged a little closer.

Elena yawned. "Uh, Asim . . ."

"Yeah?"

"I'm pretty tired."

"Oh. Okay." He shrugged. "Well, I guess the romantic evening is off then." He laughed sharply. "Just kidding."

"We do have to get up really early tomorrow," she reminded him.

"Right. Probably around five or so. The rooster won't crow until 5:45 but we'll need time to prepare."

Elena took another sip of cocoa. "Do you have an alarm clock?"

Asim shook his head. "The only alarm I need is in my head. I get up early when I'm out here. It's genetic. My special automatic brain wakes me up. "

"I see. Well, I brought an alarm clock with me just in case."

"Okay. Nice idea."

"I'm practical like that."

"I didn't know that about you." He drummed his fingers on the tray. "Look, if you want to hit the sack, no worries. I'll sit up for a while and join you later." He stuffed a large piece of muffin in his mouth.

"Well, I feel guilty, Asim. I mean, you drove me all the way out here, and now you have to stay up all by yourself."

"No worries, Elena. I'm used to it. Loneliness becomes me. By all means, go to bed."

She sighed. "I just need to use the bathroom first."

"Sure thing. No problem. Plumbing's fine, but let the water run for a minute before you use it. Uh, I'll take your tray."

"No, you don't have to."

"Really, no problem. You're the guest here."

Elena gave in and handed Asim her tray, then went into the bathroom. When she was finished washing her face and brushing her teeth, she stepped back into the little room.

"Good night, Asim."

"Night, Elena."

Elena walked into the bedroom and closed the door. It had no lock, but if she was going to undress, she needed to feel safe. It was dark, but the moon outside peeked through the windows. A curtain hung from hooks in the ceiling, separating the room into two halves. The bed next to the door had no sheets or pillows. Did she have to make her own bed?

Pushing through the curtain, Elena entered the rear of the room. She switched on the lamp beside the bed and blinked. The bed next to the window was already made and fitted with a sheet, two pillows, and a blanket. Elena shook her head. Asim had set it up for her while she was in the bathroom.

She touched the curtain. It wasn't a real barrier. It would be easy for Asim to slip through the curtain. Then he could . . . She shivered. No, Asim was a gentleman. A small voice inside her head was uneasy. How well did she really know Asim?

Elena rubbed her eyes and yawned. She was too tired to think. She took off her shoes and socks, then her pants and blouse. For a moment she sat there in her bra and panties. What if Asim walked in now? What would she do? She shivered again. Elena put on her nightgown and got into bed, pulling the blanket over her. In a few moments, she was warm and cozy.

Through the wall, she heard the faint sound of music. Asim was still up and out there alone. She guessed he was disappointed, sad, and maybe horny. He said he was a gentleman. Elena hoped he was telling the truth.

Setting the alarm clock, Elena placed it on the night table. Then she laid her head against the pillow.

* * *

Elena was fast asleep when the sound of heavy breathing woke her. Opening her eyes, she blinked. Asim stood there, his face red. She hugged the blanket and opened her mouth to scream . . .

The harsh bleep of the alarm clock shocked Elena awake. She blinked, squeezed her eyes shut, and opened them. It was a bad dream. Leaning over, she shut the alarm off. Outside, it was still dark. It was 4:00am.

She dressed, pulling on her pants and blouse. Then she pulled apart the curtain and peeked through. The mattress was still bare. Asim wasn't in the room. Stepping through the curtain, she noticed that the door was closed. Where was he?

Elena opened the door and went into the living room. The lamp was on. Asim was curled up on the couch, snoring. He was fully dressed. Elena giggled. So much for his special automatic brain.

9

Elena covered her mouth as she burst out laughing. Asim bolted upright, throwing out his arms in confusion. He fell off the couch, landing hard on his behind.

"Damn!" His face was beet red, and he looked dazed. "Elena?"

"Oh, Asim! I'm so sorry."

"Huh?" He shook himself, blinking and rubbing his eyes.

"Are you okay? I didn't mean to wake you."

Asim touched his rear and winced. "What's so funny?"

"Sorry, sorry. I shouldn't have laughed." She giggled again. "Your beanie fell off." She paused for a moment as he sat there. "Are you okay?"

"I'm okay. Just a little bruised. No harm, no foul. Good thing I have extra padding where it counts." He scratched his head. "You woke me up. What time is it?"

"Almost 4:15. Time to get started on the love potion."

"Oh my gosh! Sorry, Elena. Must have overslept."

She put her hands on her hips. "You think?"

"Sorry. I've been staying up late the last couple of nights studying." Asim got up and headed towards the bathroom.

"Studying? Studying what?"

"Real estate. For my license. I want to get into real estate sales. There's no future at Snowden and North without a paralegal certification or a law degree. I don't want to do that. I want a career where I can be my own boss and make big bucks." He yawned and scratched his head. "That's real estate. Now, excuse me. I need to use the john. Then we can head out to the barn."

"The barn?"

"First the john, then the barn."

Elena couldn't believe that Asim was studying for his license. He really did have a master plan. He always seemed so easygoing. Who would have thought?

Shrugging, she sat down on the couch and waited.

* * *

It was still dark as they trekked to the barn. It was freezing, and the wind burned Elena's cheeks. A few snow flurries fell.

"Thank goodness the snow isn't sticking. It's a bitch to walk out here in the snow and ice." Asim lugged the supplies for the love potion. Elena wanted to help, but he had insisted. "It's hard enough to walk out here in the dark when you don't know the place. If you drop any of this, the whole thing will be wasted." Elena knew he was right.

Asim said they should prepare the mixture in the barn. "That's where the rooster is. I think it's the timing that matters, but let's not chance it. The sound quality of the rooster's crow may also be important, so I want us to be as close to it as possible."

Elena sighed. "I would never have thought of that. You're a real friend, Asim. I hope you know how much I appreciate this."

"You can thank me if it works. I only hope Troy knows what a precious jewel you are."

Elena pulled her scarf over her face, pretending it was because of the wind. She knew she was blushing. Heat from her cheeks radiated down her neck and throughout her body. Precious jewel? The wave that ran through Elena threatened to overwhelm her.

"That's the barn," Asim said, flashing the beam of his light against a corrugated wall.

Near the barn was a small fenced in area. "That's the chicken coop, but at night my uncle puts the hens in the barn. There are also goats in there. Uncle had a cow, but she died a few months ago. The chickens are still sleeping so try not to make noise."

Elena tiptoed after him. There was an electric lantern by the doorway, and he turned it on. The ground was covered in sawdust, and the air smelled of animals and pee.

"Let's put everything on that work bench." He pointed to a long, sturdy looking wooden bench against the rear wall. As they walked over, a chicken squawked, flapping its wings as it hurried to get out of their way.

"Sorry, Mrs. Chicken," said Elena. She sneezed.

"Bless you. By the way, I think she's single," Asim quipped.

"Really? Aren't all hens part of the rooster's harem?"

Asim laughed. "Harem? That's exactly right. My bad. That rooster is one lucky bird. You know, in ancient Egypt, harem meant 'forbidden place.' It was the women's quarters, where men weren't allowed. Later, the pharaohs had multiple wives, known as 'the royal harem.' Too bad that's not legal here. I'd love a harem. Of course, you'd be my main wife." He winked.

"I'm all for harems," retorted Elena. "As long as women can have their own harems, with good looking guys. Then of course, you could be my main husband."

"I'll take marriage with you any way you want it," said Asim.

"What do we do now?" asked Elena, blushing.

"We get everything out and ready to mix. Then we wait for the rooster's crow."

"Will he crow just once? Or does it go on?"

"It depends. They can go on for a bit. Not to worry. We'll have more than enough time."

* * *

It happened within minutes. Elena was so stunned she stood there, frozen.

"C'mon Elena. It's time."

With Asim's help, she mixed all the ingredients together. Despite the cold, she was sweating after it was done. Outside, the darkness grayed as the sun edged over the horizon.

The color was red and gold like a king's robe. Then the chickens began clucking, and the goats started bleating. This made the rooster crow even more.

Elena put her hands over her ears. "I thought it was quiet out here," she yelled to Asim. "Why doesn't that damn rooster shut up?"

Asim chuckled. "We call it barnyard noise," he said loudly. "That rooster will stop when he's good and ready, or until I give him some feed. As soon as they wake up, they realize they're hungry. Me too!"

"Me three," replied Elena. She hadn't eaten any dinner except for the cocoa and muffins. She was starving.

They filled a jar with the love potion and carried it back to the cabin.

"It's done. Now let's have some breakfast. Then I'll introduce you to my aunt and uncle and get you home."

As they made their way back to the cabin, the rooster kept crowing. Snowflakes were falling faster now, and a light frost covered the ground. Elena took a breath, following in Asim's footprints. She wondered if the rooster knew something she didn't.

Towards the east, the horizon was dazzling.

10

As Elena took the subway to school, she checked her bag. The small vial and eye dropper were safely tucked in a small cardboard box. She couldn't wait. She wondered how Troy would react, if he would notice and spit out the coffee.

Elena was the first person to arrive in the classroom. She dropped two sugar cubes in the coffee she'd bought for Troy. Then she added a few drops of the love potion. She held up the cup and stared at the liquid. She sniffed it. Was there an odor? She shook her head.

Troy walked in a few minutes later. As usual, he tossed off his coat and sat down at the desk. When Elena handed him the coffee, he was already playing video games.

"Ah, Elena," he said, grinning. Her heart fluttered when that dimple deepened in his chin. Closing his eyes, he gulped down the coffee. "Ahh! Now that's the antidote for a hangover if ever there was one," he said, wiping his mouth on his sleeve. Pausing, he opened his eyes wide, as if startled. They glowed like blue gems.

Elena waited a moment. Troy turned to her. "That was the best coffee ever, Laynee. I feel wide awake already. And I owe it all to you." He grinned. He patted her on the arm, then squeezed it for a moment. "Thanks, kid."

Elena's brain whirled. The potion was already working. Troy had never touched her before. Her arm tingled. She was in heaven.

All day long, Elena was giddy. She kept looking at Troy. It was the most wonderful day of her life. When Asim came in, late as usual, she winked.

"You did it," he whispered.

She nodded. "Yes, I did."

Later though, when Sasha walked in, Troy was all over her.

"No worries, Elena," Asim whispered. "It takes time to work."

Asim was probably right. It would take a few days. She grinned, imagining what it would be like when Troy kissed her.

* * *

At lunch, Elena chattered to Asim like a jaybird. "Oh, Asim, he just drank the coffee in one gulp. Then, his eyes opened, so wide and blue like a robin's egg. And when he touched me . . ."

Asim sat and listened. He kept smiling.

At last, running out of air, she stopped. "It's working, Asim. The love potion's working. I can't wait for the Christmas party. Oh thank you so much for helping me. You're such a good friend." She reached out, patted him on the hand.

Asim closed his eyes and sighed. Then, leaning on his elbows, he rested his chin on his palms and gazed at her. "Wow, Elena," he said. "You're beautiful when you're in love. So beautiful." Asim's eyes were dark, shiny marbles. "Tell me more. What did Troy do?"

Pleased, Elena laughed, bubbling over with happiness. She sipped her tea, then went to the restroom. When she returned, Asim was startled as she came over, jamming his hand into his pocket. She couldn't help repeating how Troy had squeezed her arm, how dizzy she was.

Later, when they walked out together, she was so excited she didn't even notice when Asim put his arm gently around her waist.

* * *

At home that evening, Elena was walking on air. She threw out her arms and spun around.

"Elena, you are glowing." As usual, Alma sat on the carpet in lotus pose.

"Yes, my aunt, life is wonderful, and I'm in love." She spun around again.

"Tell me what happened."

She laughed. "I put the love potion in Troy's coffee. He didn't even notice. He gulped it all down. But then his eyes were big moons, harvest moons. Except they were blue. Bluer than blue! Then he squeezed my arm."

Elena took a deep breath and exhaled. "He squeezed me on the arm. I almost fainted. He is so strong. Oh Alma, it's working, it's working! The potion is working!" She spun around again.

"Easy, *chica*. All that whirling makes me dizzy. So, he touched you on the arm. I wonder what he'll touch next."

"What?"

"It's early yet, Elena. Wait before you say he is in love."

"No. I see it in your face, Auntie. You still don't believe. But now I'm sure. That old woman was a real *Curupira*. The love potion is magic. Soon, Troy will love me. Just in time for Christmas. That is the best gift Santa could ever bring."

"We will see, *chica*. We will see." Alma straightened her back. "A touch on the arm. Yes, that is no small thing. But for now, *chica*, you must shower and drink water. Then, we will continue with your yoga lessons."

Elena nodded. But she couldn't sleep, and her arm didn't stop tingling. All she could think of was Troy and his eyes, eyes like dark, shiny marbles.

11

The time flew by. Before Elena knew it, it was Christmas. Elena wore her best red dress and put up her hair. She even used some makeup when Alma wasn't looking. Glancing down at her stomach, she smiled. The yoga had made her lose weight. She couldn't wait for Troy to see her.

Carmen shuffled into the classroom. "Merry Christmas," she croaked out.

Elena nodded. The words sounded like a curse. Where was Sasha? Looking around, Elena didn't see her anywhere.

Just then, Asim walked in. He wore a new fitted suit. His tie was also new, dark red with a green fringe. On his head was a Santa beanie. Coming over to her, he bowed and took it off.

Elena stared at him, confused. He seemed taller. All his hair was gone.

"Asim. Your hair? It's gone."

"Yep." Asim rubbed his skull. It was round, a polished moonstone. He grinned. "Well, there wasn't much, Elena." He winked. "So I made lemonade out of a lemon. I shaved it all off. Now I look like a younger Vin Diesel, or Captain Picard, or even Yul Brynner. Remember Yul Brynner?"

"The King of Egypt."

"Yep. He was the man." He paused. "Now I'm the man." His voice was deep, and his dark eyes were bright.

Elena swallowed and touched her forehead. It was warm, and she was dizzy. "Excuse me a moment."

"Sure. Take your time. I'll be waiting."

In the bathroom, Elena splashed her face with cold water. She wondered where Troy was. Her cheeks were hot, and she was giddy. Was Troy hot and giddy too? She wondered if the love potion affected her as well as him.

Asim stood tall and proud as she went over to him.

"Hey, Elena, feeling better?"

"A little." She sank down into her seat and took a sip of tea. "I haven't slept for the past two weeks. The dreams . . ." She sighed. "Where's Troy? I haven't seen Sasha either. Have you seen her?"

Asim raised his eyebrows. "Didn't you hear? She quit school."

"She quit?"

"Quit or was expelled. Who knows?"

"So now Troy . . ."

"Exactly. He's all yours now."

"I see."

Just then, Troy stumbled in. He collapsed in a chair. Elena waved at him. Looking up, he noticed her and raised his hand.

"I think he's tired." Asim frowned. "Not getting enough rest. Dreaming about you, I guess. Must be the love potion." He shrugged. "Let's head over to the refreshments. I'm sure your love boat will join us in a little while."

Elena glanced at Troy, but he was holding his head.

As they walked together, Asim took Elena's hand. Confused, she let him. His hand was warm, and the contact felt good. He'd grown a beard. It was neat and trim. It looked good on him. Made him look less like a boy and more like a man. His waist was narrow and his shoulders wide.

Elena was a little dizzy. "Have you lost weight?"

Asim nodded and kept walking. Suddenly, the lights dimmed, and the decorations on the Christmas tree lit up. Asim squeezed Elena's hand. She stared at him and gasped. In the colored lights, he was handsome.

Asim stopped suddenly. "Elena, look." He pointed overhead. A wreath of mistletoe hung from the ceiling, fresh and green. "It's time. Way past time." His voice was deep.

"Time, Asim? Time for what?"

"For this." Taking Elena in his arms, Asim kissed her.

Her legs wobbled. Asim's body was strong. Flab had turned into muscle. When Asim released her, Elena was light-headed. She touched her lips. They vibrated.

"Now that's how a pretty girl should be kissed," Asim grunted. He put his hands lightly on her shoulders.

She swallowed, breathless. "What's happening?" she demanded, grabbing Asim's arm.

He grinned. "Maybe it's the magic love potion. I put it in your tea."

"What?" Elena couldn't speak.

"Excuse me." Troy staggered over.

Elena wrinkled her nose. His clothes were rumpled, and he smelled of alcohol. Elena realized he was drunk. Then it hit her. He was always drunk.

"My turn." Troy tried to push Asim aside but couldn't budge him.

"Your turn? Your turn for what?" Elena stared at Troy. His eyes were dull, and he looked sick.

"My turn to kiss you. I think I love you, Elena. I always did. Sasha was in the way." He burped. "Now she's gone."

"No." Elena shook her head as Troy moved closer.

"You're drunk, dude." Asim stepped between Troy and Elena.

Troy wobbled and lost his balance. Reaching out, Asim held him up.

"I drink too much, don't I?" Troy looked at Elena. His eyes were wide, the whites yellowed, the pupils watery blue.

She nodded. "Yes, you do."

Asim half carried Troy to a nearby chair and set him down. Troy's head sagged.

"He's asleep." Asim shrugged.

"Now what?" Elena was trembling.

"This." He kissed her lightly and stared into her eyes. "I love you, Elena."

"I love you too," she said softly. "It must be the love potion."

This time, when Asim kissed her, it went on forever.

Gift of the Curupira

12

"So, Elena, once again you are in love." Alma sat in lotus position under the Christmas tree. It was lit up now. Alma and Elena placed their Christmas gifts beneath it. The angel on top was bright and cheery.

Elena nodded. She stared at the Christmas tree with shining eyes. "Yes, Alma. This time it's real. I love Asim. It was the magic love potion that opened my eyes."

"I do not understand. Please explain, *chica*. You gave the love potion to Troy, yes?"

"Yes, I gave the potion to Troy. But while I was putting the drops in his coffee, Asim was putting drops in my tea."

"Asim used the potion too?"

Elena nodded. "It was wrong of him, I know, to put my love potion aside for his own use. But after all, he helped me make it, so maybe that's okay?"

Alma shook her head. "I see. A clever young man who took what he wanted."

Elena wrinkled her nose. "Please, Alma, don't judge Asim. He did it out of love. He did it for me."

"He did it for you?"

Elena nodded. "Yes. He loved me and saw the mistake I was making. I was blind. I did not see the true love, only the false love. Perhaps it was the *Curupira* . . ."

"Yes. The *Curupira*. No doubt." Alma nodded. "She is everywhere and spends all her time toying with my Elena."

Elena frowned. "Without the magic love potion, I would never have fallen in love with Asim. It was fate. He is my soulmate. I was blind. The magic helped me to see."

"Of course. Christmas, Asim's weight lifting, and his new hairdo had nothing to do with it."

"No. Yes." Elena waved her hands. "That was the magic love potion, too."

"Hmm." Alma lifted an eyebrow." Asim believes this too?"

"Not exactly . . . Alma, he's a guy. He says he had it planned all along."

"Planned what?"

"The Christmas party. The kiss."

"Yes. And the trip to the farm?"

Elena nodded. "That too, Auntie. Uh, Asim said he was going to use another excuse to get me up to the farm. He wanted me to see the moon and the stars. To soften me up for love." She blushed. "The love potion was an easy excuse so he used that."

"I see. He made lemonade out of a lemon."

A lemon? I don't understand. What's the lemon?"

Alma sighed. "The love potion, of course. That's the lemon, *chica*."

"No, that can't be the lemon. It worked. The *Curupira's* magic is very powerful. More powerful than you know."

Alma nodded. "Perhaps. Perhaps you are right." She stood up and walked towards the door. She was limping badly.

"Where are you going, Auntie? And why are you limping like that? What's wrong? Are you sick?" Glancing down, Elena noticed Alma's feet. They were turned backwards. Elena cried out. "You, you are the *Curupira*!"

Alma began shaking as if she was having a fit. Then her eyes crinkled, and she laughed. Balancing on one leg like an ostrich, she removed first one shoe, then the other. "You see, *chica*? This trick of the backwards feet is not so hard after all!"

Still laughing, Alma opened the front door. Asim stood there grinning.

About The Author

Sergio de Moliere lives and writes in New York City. He draws on the diversity of the vast metropolis for his characters.

About The Publisher

Story Shares is a nonprofit focused on supporting the millions of teens and adults who struggle with reading by creating a new shelf in the library specifically for them. The ever-growing collection features content that is compelling and culturally relevant for teens and adults, yet still readable at a range of lower reading levels.

Story Shares generates content by engaging deeply with writers, bringing together a community to create this new kind of book. With more intriguing and approachable stories to choose from, the teens and adults who have fallen behind are improving their skills and beginning to discover the joy of reading. For more information, visit storyshares.org.

Easy to Read. Hard to Put Down.

Gift of the Curupira